The Wood Between the Worlds

Adapted from

The Chronicles of Narnia

by C. S. Lewis

Illustrated by Deborah Maze

HarperCollins*Publishers*

A special thanks to Douglas Gresham and the C. S. Lewis Estate
for their invaluable guidance and advice in helping to create
THE WORLD OF NARNIA™ picture books.

Library of Congress Cataloging-in-Publication Data
The wood between the worlds : adapted from The chronicles of Narnia by
C. S. Lewis ; illustrated by Deborah Maze.
    p.   cm.
  "The story of The Wood Between the Worlds is based on the book The
Magician's nephew by C.S. Lewis. The Magician's nephew is one of the
seven titles in The chronicles of Narnia series written by C.S. Lewis."
  Summary: Uncle Andrew uses a set of magic rings to send Polly and his
nephew Digory into another world, where they meet the evil Queen Jadis.
  ISBN 0-06-027640-1.
  [1. Fantasy.]   I. Lewis, C. S. (Clive Staples), 1898–1963. Magician's nephew.
II. Maze, Deborah, ill.
PZ7.W8464   1999   98-17130
[Fic]—DC21   CIP
                                                                   AC

1   2   3   4   5   6   7   8   9   10
❖
First Edition

For Douglas and Merrie

Long ago, there lived in London a girl called Polly Plummer. She lived in one of a long row of houses which were all joined together. One morning when she was in her garden, she met her neighbor, a boy named Digory, who had come to London with his sick mother to live with his aunt and uncle while his father was in India.

Polly and Digory met nearly every day. When it was raining, they had to find indoor things to do. Polly had a little secret "cave" up in the attic, and they soon realized they could travel the whole length of the row of houses, in the roof space. One day, while exploring the attic, they found a little door, opened it, and saw that they were looking into a furnished room. There was a table in the middle of the room piled with all sorts of things. But what Polly noticed first was a tray of yellow and green rings. They were beautiful.

Suddenly, a chair in front of the fireplace moved and there rose up out of it Digory's Uncle Andrew. They were in Digory's house, and in his uncle's forbidden study! Uncle Andrew walked to the door and turned the key in the lock. He smiled and said, "I am delighted to see you. You see, I'm in the middle of a great experiment."

"Look here, Uncle Andrew," said Digory, "you must let us out."

"Very well. But I must give you a present before you go," said Uncle Andrew, and he offered Polly a yellow ring.

"Polly!" shouted Digory. "Don't touch it!"

It was too late. Just as he spoke, Polly's hand touched the ring, and immediately, without a flash or a noise or a warning of any sort, there was no Polly.

"My experiment has succeeded," said Uncle Andrew. "The little girl's vanished right out of the world."

"What *do* you mean?" asked Digory.

"Long ago, my godmother gave me a box that was filled with magic dust. It had come from the lost island of Atlantis. After many failed experiments, I succeeded in making these rings from the dust. The yellow rings will send any creature that touches them into an Other Place. The green rings will bring you back."

"But Polly hasn't got a green ring," said Digory.

"She can get back," said Uncle Andrew, "if someone else will go after her with a green ring."

And now Digory saw the trap in which he was caught.

"All right," said Digory angrily. "I have to go after her. What must I do?"

"The moment you touch a yellow ring, you vanish out of this world," explained Uncle Andrew. "When you are in the Other Place, I expect that the moment you touch a green ring, you vanish out of that world and reappear in this. Now take these two greens—one for you and one for Polly. And pick up a yellow one for yourself."

Digory took a deep breath and picked up the rings.

The next thing Digory knew, he was standing at the edge of a pool in a very quiet wood. There were dozens of other pools, one every few yards. The strangest thing was that Digory had half forgotten how he had come there. After a long time, he noticed that there was a girl a short distance away.

"I think I've seen you before," she said dreamily.

"I rather think so too," said Digory.

And then, at exactly the same moment, they knew who they were and began to remember the whole story.

"How do we get home?" said Polly.

"Go back into the pool, I expect," answered Digory.

They took hands, stood at the edge of the pool, and jumped. But when they opened their eyes, they found they were still standing in the pool in that green wood.

"What on earth's gone wrong?" said Polly.

"Oh! I know," said Digory. "We're still wearing our yellow rings. They're for the outward journey. The green ones take you home."

But before they tried another jump, Digory suggested that they try to go somewhere else by jumping into one of the other pools.

"I'm not going to try any new pool till we've made sure that we *can* get back by the old one," said Polly.

So they decided to test it. They put on the green rings and jumped back into the same pool. Almost at once, they could see rows of roofs and chimneys and St. Paul's Cathedral and knew they were looking at London. Then Polly shouted "Change!" and London faded away, and the green light above grew stronger till their heads came out of the pool. They scrambled ashore, and Digory made a mark in the grass beside the pool so they would always be able to recognize it as the one that would take them home.

"Now for the adventure!" said Digory.

They walked over to the edge of another pool with their yellow rings on, and once more they jumped.

But again, it didn't work.

"What's gone wrong now?" exclaimed Digory. "Uncle Andrew said yellow for the outward journey." Then they decided to try their green rings, just to see what would happen. This time it worked. A moment later, they noticed a dull, red light. They were standing in a sort of courtyard. The sky was almost black. They went out of that courtyard into a doorway, and up a great flight of steps and through huge rooms. Finally, they came to two doors. One stood a little ajar. They went to look in.

The room was full of figures, all sitting perfectly still. They had robes and crowns and precious stones round their necks. All the faces Polly and Digory could see looked kind and wise. But after they had gone a few steps, they came to faces that looked more solemn. Farther on, they found themselves among strong, proud, but cruel faces.

The last figure of all was a woman even more richly dressed than the others, very tall, with a look of fierceness and pride. Yet she was beautiful too.

"I do wish we knew the story behind all this," said Digory. "Let's go back and look at that table sort of thing in the middle of the room."

The thing in the middle of the room was a square pillar. On it, there rose a golden arch from which there hung a little golden bell, and beside it lay a little golden hammer. On the side of the pillar was written:

Make your choice, adventurous Stranger;
Strike the bell and bide the danger,
Or wonder, till it drives you mad,
What would have followed if you had.

Digory very much wanted to ring the bell, and even though Polly was firmly against it, he leaned forward and struck it. The bell gave out a note that grew louder, and then great blocks of masonry began to fall around them.

"There! I hope you're satisfied now," said Polly.

"Well, it's all over, anyway," said Digory.

He could not have been more wrong.

Suddenly, they noticed that the beautiful woman was rising from her chair. You could see at once that she was a great queen.

"Who has awaked me?" she asked.

"I think it must have been me," said Digory.

"How did such as you dare to enter this house?" she asked.

"We've come from another world; by Magic," said Polly.

"But you are no Magician," said the Queen to Digory. "It is on another's Magic that you traveled here."

"It was my Uncle Andrew," said Digory.

At that moment, there came a roar of falling masonry, and the floor shook.

"The palace is collapsing. Come, or we shall be buried in the ruin," said the Queen.

The Queen led them through a maze of halls, stairs, and courtyards, until they came to a large hall. At the far end were two heavy doors fastened with great bars, too high to reach and too heavy to lift. The Queen raised her arm, said something they couldn't understand, and those heavy doors crumbled away and became a heap of dust.

"Remember what you have seen," said the Queen. "This is what happens to things and people that stand in my way."

The Queen led them out onto a terrace, and below them there spread a vast city with no living thing in it. Near the horizon hung a great, red sun.

"Such was the great city of Charn," said the Queen. "It is silent now. I, Jadis, the last Queen, but the Queen of the World, blotted it out forever. Now, let us be going," said the Queen.

"Going where?" asked both the children.

"To your world, of course," answered Jadis.

"I'm sure you wouldn't like our world at all," said Digory, looking fearfully at Polly. "It's not worth seeing, really."

"It will be worth seeing when I rule it," answered the Queen.

"But you can't!" said Digory. "They wouldn't let you."

"Foolish boy! Do you think that I will not have your world at my feet before a year has passed?" said the Queen.

"Perhaps you fear for this uncle of yours, but I am not coming to fight against *him*. Is he King of your whole world or only of part?"

"He isn't King of anywhere," said Digory.

"You are lying," said the Queen. "Who ever heard of common people being Magicians? Your uncle is the great King of your world."

"Well, not *exactly*," said Digory.

"Minions!" cried the Queen as she lunged for Polly.

"Now!" shouted Digory. They touched their yellow rings, and that dreary world vanished. Then their heads came out of the pool and into the quietness of the Wood between the Worlds. But they were not alone. The Queen had come up with them, holding on to Polly's hair. In the wood, Queen Jadis looked much paler and seemed to be finding it hard to breathe. Neither of the children was afraid of her now.

"Let go of her hair!" shouted Digory at the Queen.

And they forced her to let Polly's hair go.

"Quick! Change rings and into the home pool," said Polly.

But as they jumped, Digory felt a large cold finger and thumb had caught him by the ear. He struggled and kicked, but it was no use.

In a moment, they found themselves in Uncle Andrew's study. There was Uncle Andrew himself, staring at Queen Jadis. Polly and Digory stared at her too, for the Witch had gotten over her faintness and once again looked fierce, terrifying, and beautiful. And although Digory and Polly didn't know it right then, the adventures that would lead them to the land of Narnia had only just begun.

ETTINSMOOR

RIVER SHRIBBLE

THE GREAT RIVER

RIVER RUSH

RIVER

Glasswater

A MAP OF NARNIA